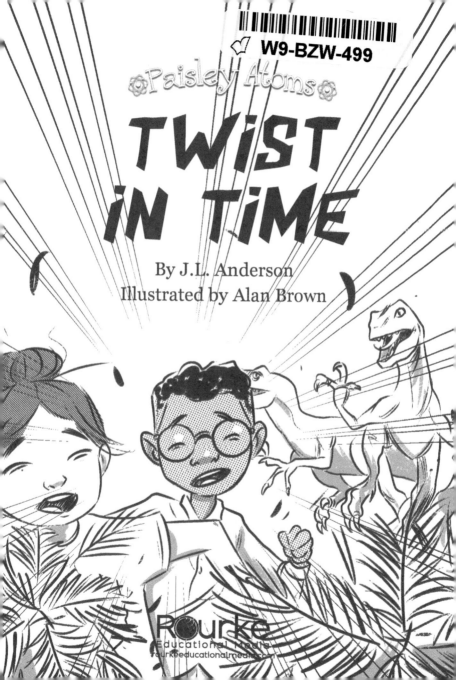

www.rourkeeducationalmedia.com

Edited by: Keli Sipperley
Cover and Interior layout by: Rhea Magaro-Wallace
Cover and Interior Illustrations by: Alan Brown

Library of Congress PCN Data

Twist in Time / J.L. Anderson
(Paisley Atoms)
ISBN (hard cover)(alk. paper) 978-1-68191-720-7
ISBN (soft cover) 978-1-68191-821-1
ISBN (e-Book) 978-1-68191-916-4
Library of Congress Control Number: 2016932598

Printed in the United States of America,
North Mankato, Minnesota
01-0272313053

Dear Parents and Teachers,

Future world-famous scientist Paisley Atoms and her best friend, Ben Striker, aren't afraid to stir things up in their quests for discovery. Using Paisley's basement as a laboratory, the two are constantly inventing, exploring, and, well, making messes. Paisley has a few bruises to show for their work, too. She wears them like badges of honor.

These fast-paced adventures weave fascinating facts, quotes from real scientists, and explanations for various phenomena into witty dialogue, stealthily boosting your reader's understanding of multiple science topics. From sound waves to dinosaurs, from the sea floor to the moon, Paisley, Ben and the gang are perfect partner resources for a STEAM curriculum.

Each illustrated chapter book includes a science experiment or activity, a biography of a woman in science, jokes, and websites to visit.

In addition, each book also includes online teacher/parent notes with ideas for incorporating the story into a lesson plan. These notes include subject matter, background information, inspiration for maker space activities, comprehension questions, and additional online resources. Notes are available at: www.RourkeEducationalMedia.com.

We hope you enjoy Paisley and her pals as much as we do.

Happy reading,
Rourke Educational Media

TABLE OF CONTENTS

Dinosaur Craze..6

Outrageous Ideas.......................................16

Time Travel Machine Mayhem...........................25

Dangerous Dino-Discovering 34

Eureka! 45

CHAPTER ONE
DINOSAUR CRAZE

Paisley had an active imagination, but even she had a hard time imagining that a farmer would've found dinosaur fossils only thirty-eight miles from Roarington.

Dinosaur fossils right at the diamond-shaped base of Roaring Mountain!

"This is epic news," her best friend, Ben, said.

Paisley tried to picture dinosaurs roaming around prehistoric Roarington. Paleontologists were studying the fossils at the university to find out more. Paisley hoped her dad would get some inside details since he was a biologist there.

The kids at Roarington Elementary went wild about the dinosaur discovery. The principal, Mrs. Proton, even led a campus dig for the fifth grade students before school started. Suki and Sumi dressed up in matching safari outfits, though they didn't want to get dirty.

The perfectionist Whitney-Raelynn surprised Paisley when she dug a hole with her bare hands. "I'll find the most complete dinosaur skeleton in history," she said.

Ben dug a little faster.

Whitney-Raelynn's fancy sweater was covered in more dirt than Paisley's T-shirt. Paisley took pride that she had a bruise on her shoulder from her crazy adventures that Whitney-Raelynn didn't have.

"Dinosaurs can't come back to life the way they do in the movies, can they?" Arjun asked as he uncovered something white and solid.

"RRRrrroooar!" Rosalind yelled as she wheeled up behind him.

"Aaaaah!" Arjun screamed. He ran away from the rock he was digging up with a speed that might've rivaled the ostrich-like dinosaur, *Dromiceiomimus*.

Rosalind laughed so hard she had a coughing fit.

That was the most exciting part of the dig since no one had any luck finding fossils. Paisley planned on digging in her backyard with Ben later. Too bad his was mostly concrete between the porch and the swimming pool.

Once the morning bell rang, the teachers at Roarington Elementary assigned all kinds of school projects about dinosaurs. Paisley and Ben had to read dinosaur books, write dinosaur stories, and Mrs. Decibel even had them sing dinosaur songs.

"For your next project, you'll create a model of what you think the dinosaur might've looked like," Mrs. Beaker, the science teacher, said.

"These terrible lizards are going to give me a lifetime of nightmares," Arjun said.

Paisley laughed, but not as loud as Rosalind.

The word *dinosaur* meant *terrible lizard*, though they weren't actually lizards. Paisley didn't think they were terrible either.

Paisley and Ben got started on their dinosaur models after digging around in her backyard after school. Newton, Paisley's pet mongoose, thought digging holes in the grass was great fun. Newton pounced and dined on grub worms until his tummy bloated.

"Too bad we can't dig in the Pendleburys' backyard," Paisley said. When she peeked over their neighbor's fence, she caught the little girl, Mia, spying on them. They waved at her and she ran off.

Dad had dinosaur veggie nuggets waiting for Paisley and Ben once they cleaned up, just like he used to make when they were the same age as Mia.

"Why did we ever outgrow our dinosaur phase?" Paisley asked as she dipped one of the nuggets in ranch dressing.

"I'm not sure we did exactly. We just buried it with a lot of other new phases," Ben said. He pulled out one of his old dog-eared dinosaur encyclopedias from his backpack. He and Paisley used to read it out loud together to memorize facts, like how some dinosaurs were as small as chickens *(Compsognathus)* or as long as five double-decker buses *(Seismosaurus)*.

"True, though we aren't as obsessed as we used to be," Paisley said. She laughed thinking about how Dad had sewed them dinosaur blankets and Mom trimmed a hedge out front to look like an *Allosaurus*. Their neighbors, Mr. and Mrs. Pendlebury, forced them to cut it down after Halloween because they thought it looked tacky.

After eating, Dad showed Paisley and Ben a replica of the fossils found near Roaring Mountain. "It pays to have paleontologist friends at the university," Dad said.

Paisley knew she could count on him!

Dad held up the fossil replica. "See how there is a hole in the hip socket? This feature sets dinosaurs apart. It helped dinosaurs stand upright. Otherwise, their legs would be out to the side like other reptiles."

"Did it help dinosaurs run faster?" Ben asked.

"Exactly," Dad said.

Newton climbed on Paisley's shoulder after sniffing the replica. Paisley was surprised to find the bones were hollow and the walls of the bones were thin. It was like Dad could read her mind.

"This indicates it was a theropod, one of the carnivorous, beast-footed dinosaurs," Dad said. "A specialized group of theropods developed the ability to fly, though there is some mystery as to whether they learned to fly from the ground up or from the trees down. We know theropods as birds today." He lit up as he spoke like he'd never outgrown his dinosaur phase from childhood, either.

Mom was the same way when Paisley video chatted with her later. She usually wore a flower pushed behind her ear, but tonight, she wore a glittery dinosaur hair clip. Newton clawed at the screen, it was so shiny.

"Hi, *mija*. Such exciting news happening in Roarington," Mom said, "and here in Mexico, too."

Mom was on a research project in Mexico, trying to find the thought-to-be-extinct chocolate cosmos growing in the wild. The chocolate cosmos was a beautiful burgundy flower that smelled like chocolate. She told Paisley about a dinosaur graveyard discovered close to her lodge. "Some of the dinosaurs even had fossilized feathers," Mom said. "Anyway, I wish I was there to help you out with your science project."

"Thanks, Mom! You've actually given me some great ideas."

"Happy dino-discovering, *mija*," Mom said, which was kind of cheesy, but it made Paisley smile.

When Ben returned that evening, Paisley couldn't wait to work on the dinosaur model. They went to their lab in Paisley's basement to craft a skeleton based on the replica of the fossils. They used toilet paper and paper towel tubes for the bones.

Next, they added some muscles using modeling clay. After Dad went on and on about dinosaur traits, they made sure to create jaw muscles that reached the top of the skull.

"This is going to be the most accurate dinosaur model in our class," Paisley said.

"And the most artistic," Ben said with a yawn. Newton was curled up in his lap, snoring.

It was getting late as they formed the skin out of recycled plastic trash bags. Their dinosaur model still needed some paint and details when Dad popped his head into their lab. "Bedtime soon!" he said. "You both need to wrap it up for the night."

"Oh man, I better get home before my parents come over and drag me out," Ben said. His parents worked from their home next-door to the Atoms house. They really had dragged him home from the lab before. Well, his father picked him up and carried him. He was a bit smaller back then.

"We're so close to finishing," Paisley said, fighting a yawn. "You don't think we could add some paint and details really quick?"

"You can paint if you want to, but we have a big day of dinosaurs ahead of us tomorrow," Ben said.

Paisley laughed thinking about the dinosaur songs Mrs. Decibel had them sing.

After Ben left, the local newspaper called Dad to get his opinion on the fossil discovery.

Paisley planned to just add a few minor details to their project, but she got a little carried away. Actually, a lot carried away.

Ben was right about the artistic part, and Paisley hoped he wouldn't be upset with her.

CHAPTER TWO
OUTRAGEOUS IDEAS

Paisley had their dinosaur model covered when Ben met her for their morning walk to school.

"Did you paint it?" Ben asked.

Paisley nodded, then tried distracting him with plans about sneaking into the Pendleburys' yard to look for fossils.

"I could help you," Mia said as she jumped out from behind a fence post.

"Eek!" Paisley shrieked. She nearly dropped their model. "Please don't scare us like that. You shouldn't be spying either."

"Sorry," Mia said. She was wearing an outfit just like Paisley's.

"Can I see the model?" Ben asked.

"Sure, when we get to school. It seems like it might start drizzling," she said.

Ben either wasn't paying attention to the mostly sunny sky or maybe he was worried about Paisley dropping the model because he let it go.

Paisley kept it covered until the big reveal in science class. The entire class created interesting dinosaur models. Rosalind's model looked more like a monster than a dinosaur. She teased Arjun with it.

Arjun made a *Diplododus*, a long-necked, long-tailed dinosaur.

"That's awesome," Paisley said, "though this type of dinosaur is a sauropod instead of a theropod." She shared what her dad had said about the theropod bones and the bird connection.

Arjun crossed his arms. "I'm no science genius like you, but at least this dinosaur ate plants and wasn't scary."

"There are still a lot of unanswered questions about dinosaurs, and the point of the models was to exercise our imaginations," Mrs. Beaker said, giving Paisley a stern look.

Paisley shrank in her seat and kept her comments to herself when Suki and Sumi showed off their model, a *Pteranodon*. The students murmured their appreciation.

"What a wonderful dinosaur model," Mrs. Beaker said.

Paisley couldn't stay quiet any longer. "Actually, a *Pteranodon* is a flying reptile that lived during the time of dinosaurs. Dinosaurs roamed on land."

Mrs. Beaker gave Paisley another look. Paisley zipped it.

"Can you believe that?" Paisley whispered to Ben. He shrugged it off.

Whitney-Raelynn created a *Velociraptor* that looked realistic with snake-like camouflage-colored skin.

The class applauded, and Whitney-Raelynn took a bow.

Paisley kept her arms crossed and her lips zipped

until she and Ben presented their model.

The class gasped when she took the cover off—no one louder than Ben. "You gave our *Tyrannosaurus rex* blue feathers?"

"Iridescent blue, and only in a few logical places," Paisley said.

"A jungle green *T. rex* with blue feathers seems more like a cartoon model," Rosalind said.

Suki and Sumi giggled.

"If you are so worried about dinosaur accuracy, Paisley, then why didn't you make your model look more accurate?" Whitney-Raelynn asked.

Mrs. Beaker nodded her head in agreement.

Paisley huffed even though she predicted a response like this. "I personally think I did. Since there aren't any fossilized skin samples, we can only guess. A study was done a while ago showing that protein from *T. rex* bones helped prove a connection between dinosaurs and modern birds."

"A relative of the *T. rex* had featherlike additions, so it isn't out of the question," Ben said. "Scientists

also found a bloodthirsty peacock-like dinosaur."

"Hmm," Mrs. Beaker said.

Paisley could tell their science teacher wasn't convinced. She also could've hugged her best friend. She wished there was some way they could go back in time to prove that she wasn't wrong.

"You're not mad at me, are you?" Paisley asked Ben on their walk home after school.

"Shocked at first, I guess," Ben said. "I just wish you would've showed me the model beforehand so I would've been prepared."

"That wasn't fair of me," Paisley said. "I didn't want you to be upset since I didn't clear my imagination with you first."

"I shouldn't have left you with the rest of the work," Ben said. He held out his hand and Paisley shook it. "We're good," he said.

"We'd be even better if we could prove our points," Paisley said. "If we could go back in time to the Mesozoic era with a camera, we'd REALLY amaze Roarington Elementary and the entire world."

Ben squinted as if he were thinking, or maybe even trying to see the past. Paisley knew she had him interested.

"We don't have much to lose," Ben said. After a moment he added, "I suppose our lives if things go wrong."

"Nothing will go wrong," Paisley said.

Mia somehow beat Paisley and Ben home. She waved at them while she dug around the front yard. "There is a lot of cool stuff here," she said.

"I bet," Paisley said. "Thanks for not sneaking up on us."

"You could help me—" Mia started to say.

"Sorry, but we've got important plans," Ben said, cutting her off.

Mia pouted as she went back to digging by the tree. Paisley hoped Mrs. Pendlebury wouldn't get too upset about the yard or Mia's filthy clothes.

When Paisley and Ben got to their lab, they drew up some plans for a time travel machine.

"What would be big enough that we could fit in?"

Paisley asked.

"A refrigerator," Ben said. The same thought had crossed Paisley's mind. "You think your parents would be okay with us borrowing it?"

Paisley thought for a moment. "They are pretty dedicated to science. You saw how Dad is all gaga for dinosaurs."

Ben didn't argue with that.

If everything went smoothly, they'd travel to the Mesozoic Era and and then return in time for dinner.

CHAPTER THREE
TiME TRAVEL
MACHiNE MAYHEM

The fridge was nice...for a fridge. It was extra wide and had stainless steel doors. There wasn't much food inside it after Dad's recent cooking frenzy. Paisley moved most of what was left into a cooler.

Ben did the same thing for the freezer section, which mostly held a bag of ice and some frozen mealworms. The ice would help keep the refrigerator items cool. Newton got a frosty mealworm treat.

Paisley and Ben set the camera with digital recording features inside the butter compartment. Then they unplugged the fridge and used furniture sliders to move it outside to warm up while they prepared it for time travel.

But how? Neither of them had experience building a time travel machine.

Ben tinkered with a valve in the freezer section and sighed. "Stephen Hawking said black holes are time machines."

"A black hole isn't practical right now," Paisley said as she checked out the compressor on the back side of the fridge.

Ben chuckled. "That's exactly what Stephen Hawking said, but we have your ancient key to jump start things."

The ancient key had activated many amazing adventures for them. Paisley ran her fingers over the ridges of the key and thought of her mother, who had given it to her. Mom would be really interested in dinosaur fashion like colorful wings and feathers, but mostly she would be interested in plants from the past.

"The power of the key has to work," Paisley said.

They walked inside the fridge and pressed the key

against the expansion valve in the freezer. "Please let us visit the Mesozoic era," she requested.

The fridge was cramped and the compartments made it hard for Paisley to bump her fist against Ben's. They had to twist their arms to reach. Bump. "Science Alliance!" they chanted.

Unlike many of their past adventures when they followed similar steps, nothing happened.

Paisley stepped out of the fridge and pressed the key into a notch in the compressor. They tried the fist-bump again, harder this time. "Science Alliance!"

Still, nothing.

"Maybe we aren't visiting the past for the right reasons since we want to prove people wrong," Paisley said. She didn't exactly understand the way the key worked...or didn't work.

"Learning more about dinosaurs will help us fix the model, if needed, and it will help everyone understand more," Ben said. "We all have a lot to learn with so many unanswered questions." He took off the watch he'd built and attached it to the compressor. He'd built the watch after studying Benjamin Banneker, the amazing scientist he was named after.

The watch was special, but it didn't jump them back in time.

"You promise you're not upset with me that I went a little wild with our model?" Paisley asked.

"Maybe at first," Ben said, "but then I thought it was brilliant the more I looked at it."

"Thanks for being such a good friend," she said.

"I have room for improvement," Ben said. "I also have an idea since the fridge may be too cold. I read about an experiment recently." He went back to the lab and grabbed some steel wool. Paisley helped him soak it in vinegar and then they set it in the ice compartment near the expansion valve. A chemical reaction happened as the vinegar removed the coating on the steel wool. This did nothing for time travel, though the fridge warmed up as the steel wool rusted.

Paisley wasn't ready to give up, even if she felt a little "loser-tastic" as Whitney-Raelynn might say. She petted Newton for a moment while she thought things through.

"I know!" she said, jumping up.

Newton chattered as Paisley ran into the house to find the fossil replica. Perhaps it had some sort of energy from the actual dinosaur fossil that could make their time travel adventures possible. She pressed it into the valve.

The refrigerator hummed as if it was plugged back in, but then nothing happened after that. The key felt cold and lifeless in Paisley's hand.

"We might need the actual fossil," Paisley said. How would they borrow it from the university? It was a long trip away and the fossil would be protected.

"I think we have to give up on the time travel. We'll have to rely on our imaginations instead," Ben said.

"Wait!" a voice called out.

"Mia, is that you?" Paisley asked as she looked over the fence. "Are you spying on us again?"

"Of course! You have so much more fun than me," Mia said.

Paisley wasn't sure what to say about that since they really did have a lot of fun together. She couldn't imagine life as a Pendlebury.

"Do you think this is a rock or a dinosaur tooth?" Mia asked.

Paisley reached through a wooden slat in the fence. Mia placed the object in her hand. It was oval shaped and about three inches long. The object had some fracture lines and was darker and polished on the end.

"Mia, I think you found a tooth!"

Even through the fence, Paisley could see Mia smiling. "A dinosaur tooth?" she asked.

"Either a dinosaur tooth or a Bigfoot tooth," Ben said.

"You can borrow it if you want," Mia said.

She's an okay kid, Paisley thought. "We'll bring it back," she said.

That seemed to make Mia happy enough.

Paisley tried something different and pressed the tooth and the key near a notch in the water dispenser before crawling back inside. It sure was cramped in there.

The fridge made a click-click-clicking noise after Paisley and Ben bumped fists and yelled, "Science Alliance!"

The fridge hummed again. The life force of the tooth perhaps combined with the steel wool/vinegar combo by the valve, the watch by the compressor, and the power of the ancient key seemed to be working.

"Please let us visit the Mesozoic era," Paisley asked.

Light and warmth filled the fridge. So did a stinky

vinegar smell from Ben's experiment. Something else stunk but Paisley couldn't figure out what the odor was.

"I hope Bigfoot wasn't alive back then," Ben said, "or else we're about to go on a very different mission."

She felt a rush in her stomach even before the fridge catapulted them back in time.

CHAPTER FOUR
DANGEROUS
DINO-DISCOVERING

The ride was even scarier than the Terrorizing Tower ride at the amusement park, especially since they were sandwiched in the fridge and couldn't see where they were going.

Paisley wasn't sure about the black hole theory, but she imagined that the fridge was falling through one. At least that's how it felt.

If Paisley and Ben had spent more time preparing their time travel machine, they would've added landing gear and a control panel. The fridge crashed to the ground. That was going to leave some bruises.

The fridge door creaked open.

"You okay, Paisley?" Ben asked.

"Yeah," she said, wondering what would await them when they crawled out of the fridge.

Ben crawled out first, then helped Paisley. A wave of warmth and humidity blasted them. The sky was pinkish-orange, as if the sun was starting to set.

Paisley gasped for air.

"It's the extra carbon dioxide from the volcanoes," Ben tried to say, though it took him a moment for his lungs to adapt.

Paisley's lungs adjusted and then her eyes.

Whoa!

Mom might've passed out seeing so many of the giant plants and trees. Evergreens taller than redwood trees towered above them. Jungle-like plants and ferns grew as far as she could see.

"Ooh, look at these horsetails," Paisley said, studying a plant that looked like it had layers of candleholders. "We better grab our camera. Ben?" she said, turning around.

Paisley realized why Ben was suddenly so quiet. The plants weren't the only living things greeting them. There was a welcoming committee.

Dinosaurs! Real. Live. Dinosaurs.

Paisley couldn't breathe again and it had nothing to do with the carbon dioxide in the air.

Ben's eyes were wide and she knew he was just as stunned.

These dinosaurs were the size of a Great Dane. Paisley noticed they were the same color of the horsetails mixed with some patches of brown. They were covered with bristles and fuzz. Were feathers starting to grow in? Were these baby dinosaurs?

"They're theropods," Paisley said. "Meat eaters!"

Ben took a step back to grab a camera but one of the dinosaurs snarled and lunged forward.

"Watch out, Ben!" Paisley screamed as another leaped toward him.

Ben tumbled on the ground and the dinosaur stood on his chest, licking its lips. Paisley didn't need her best friend to calculate how many seconds it would be until he was lunch.

Paisley pulled out one of the trays in the fridge, making something crash. The noise startled the dinosaurs.

"Leave him alone!" Paisley cried and swung the tray at the giant-dog-sized dinosaur that pinned Ben.

She swung it again. *Smack!* A ... direct hit on the nose!

It yelped and ran off. Paisley helped Ben to his feet. "Thanks."

The other three dinosaurs flocked to the fridge. They licked hungrily at something inside.

It was some forgotten spaghetti leftovers. *No wonder the fridge had been extra stinky*, Paisley thought.

One of the dinosaurs clawed at a pickle jar and bottles of mustard and ketchup Paisley forgot to take out. Oops.

Maybe Paisley could sneak up to get the camera. She took a few steps toward the fridge, but one of the dinosaurs zeroed in on her. It crouched down as if preparing to pounce.

"Forget it!" Ben cried. "RUN!"

Paisley had no idea where to go, but she bolted down a dirt path. She was dizzy from the time travel, the odd atmosphere, and the encounter.

If she slowed down, she'd be dino-chow. Future scientists or little kids digging in backyards might find her fossils wondering how she got there.

Just when they thought they'd ditched the dinosaurs, the beasts rounded the corner. Those special hips made them lightning fast.

"There!" Paisley said to Ben, pointing at an evergreen in the clearing they could climb.

As they got close, something screeched like a mountain lion. Paisley was afraid to look up. The reptile in the sky had a wingspan as long as a moving truck.

"A *Pteranodon*," Ben said in awe.

Unlike Suki and Sumi's model, this one had a giant crest at the top of the skull. It screeched again. The dinosaur pack chasing Paisley and Ben shrank back from the noise. But only for a second.

Paisley reached an evergreen just as one of the dinosaurs snarled at her heels. "GO AWAY!" she bellowed.

These particular dinosaurs seemed very sensitive to noise. Ben sounded like a caveman as he yelled at them, too.

The creatures shrank back. This gave Paisley a moment to scale up a tall branch. Ben scrambled up behind her.

The small, fierce dinosaurs jumped at the tree.

"Think they can climb?" Paisley asked Ben.

"Even if they're not climbers, they could probably find a way to get into the tree if they really wanted to," Ben said.

Paisley made enough noise that the dinosaurs scurried off, hopefully for good. She and Ben climbed higher into the safety of the branches.

The ground thudded as something moved in their direction. Their tree shook and Paisley held on tight to a branch.

"Open your eyes," Ben said.

Paisley hadn't realized she'd even closed them. "Whoa!"

A *Diplodocus* had reached its neck up to the tree limb and stared right at them. The sauropod's eyes reminded Paisley of a cow's for some reason. The dinosaur was light brown with darker brown spines running down its back.

The sauropod tilted its head as it studied the two kids. Then it made a noise that sounded an awful lot like a hiccup.

"Sorry if we scared you with all of our screaming," Paisley said. She pulled off a small branch of the tree and passed it to the *Diplododus*. It chomped the entire branch in one bite.Then it lumbered off. Paisley was prepared for the tree to shake this time.

Ben's stomach growled. Paisley was hungry, too, but she was more worried about being something's meal herself.

"This might not have been one of my best ideas," Paisley said. She swatted away a bug that looked like a giant flea.

"Maybe it is dangerous here, but did you see that *Pteranodon*, Paisley?"

"I wish we had recording equipment," she said.

Ben nodded. "No kidding. No one will believe we had an up close encounter with a sauropod. You even fed it!" he said. "People would pay a fortune for this kind of opportunity."

An eerie cry filled the air as if something was being attacked.

"True, but I would pay a fortune to avoid being eaten," Paisley said.

CHAPTER FIVE
EUREKA!

"I think Arjun would be having his third heart attack by now," Paisley said.

You would've thought she'd told the funniest joke ever the way Ben laughed. "I'm glad we live in modern times."

"I hope we can get back home," Paisley said.

The sun continued to lower in the sky. It was now purplish-pink. It reflected over a diamond shaped crater filled with water. "You think that's the future Roaring

Mountain?" Paisley asked.

"It's possible," Ben said.

They may have been visiting the past millions of years before their own time, but the sunset looked the same.

As they debated what to do before night fell, they watched the ancient world around them. A leathery looking theropod chased a smaller one with feathers. Just as the bigger one almost took a bite out of the smaller one, the feathery theropod jumped to escape. It used its feathers to stay airborne longer before getting away.

"That was close," Paisley said.

"That's like the mystery your dad talked about," Ben said. "Did dinosaurs learn to fly from jumping out of trees or flapping on the ground? I think dinosaurs that could stay in the air longer could live longer and this turned into full-on flying."

"I hope we get to tell Dad about our discovery," Paisley said. She hadn't even told him goodbye before they time traveled. He would see the missing fridge

and wonder what happened to them. Mia might try to explain, but they'd be twisted in time forever.

A *Seismosaurus* whipped its tail way off in the distance, creating a sonic boom that nearly knocked Paisley and Ben out of the tree.

"I really don't want to spend the night out here," Paisley said. She flicked off another giant flea.

"Me neither," said Ben.

Paisley also didn't want to run into the pack of hungry junior dinosaurs on the way back to the refrigerator. Ben kept guard as they walked-jogged back. She only stopped when she found a large gray feather and stuffed it into her pocket.

Mom always brought Paisley home something from one of her trips, so Paisley broke off a piece of the horsetail for her.

Something scuttled nearby in a piney shrub.

"Did you hear that?" Paisley whispered.

"Yeah. We should load up immediately." Ben reached the fridge first. The camera was smashed. The jar of pickles was, too. Splattered ketchup and mustard made the ground look like a battle zone.

"Ahhh!" Paisley was almost to the fridge when a dinosaur hopped out of the shrub as if it had been tracking them.

A theropod!

A theropod with iridescent blue feathers along the neck!

"Eureka!" Paisley said. It was the same color blue that she'd painted the *T. rex* model. There was no way she'd be able to get a picture of it, but maybe she could pluck a feather from its neck. Maybe theropods could be nice like the sauropod she fed. Paisley stepped forward, wishing she had a snack to offer it in exchange for a feather.

"What are you doing?" Ben yelled. "Get in the fridge!"

Paisley was about to take another step forward to steal a feather when the theropod flashed a mouthful of razor-sharp teeth. She remembered what Ben had said

about a bloodthirsty peacock-like dinosaur.

No blue feather was worth risking her life. Paisley could know she was right without having to go to an extreme. Being right seemed far less important than being alive.

The brightly colored theropod screeched.

Paisley jumped back in the fridge. She barely had time to shut the door before the beast attacked. The claws scraped the stainless steel door.

Paisley held out the key. "Get us out of here! We're done being in the Mesozoic Era."

Nothing happened right away. Did the dinosaurs destroy their time machine?

The blue-feathered dino scratched against the steel again. How long before it figured out how to open the doors?

"Please, please, send us home," Paisley begged.

The fridge click-click-clicked and then hummed. Traveling forward in time proved to be like another ride on the Terrorizing Tower.

Crash! They landed back in Paisley's yard.

Paisley helped Ben out of the fridge this time. Her lungs had to readjust all over again. Newton jumped at her as if he hadn't seen her in millions of years. The little mongoose sniffed them all over.

"I can't believe we made it out of there alive," Ben said. He sounded like he'd sucked helium out of a balloon.

Mia stood right by the fence in the same spot as she had before they'd left. "How did you do that trick?" she asked.

"Trick?" Paisley asked.

"The fridge was okay a second ago. Now it is all beat up and you have scratches," Mia said.

Paisley looked at the fridge. It was indeed beat up with deep claw gouges, and they had several scratches. Yes, she had an active imagination, but she hadn't imagined their adventure. Ben scratched his head like he was taking in the whole experience, too.

Paisley's muscles felt like goo as she grabbed the dinosaur tooth fossil and walked toward Mia. "Thanks for letting us borrow this," she said. Paisley thought about giving the feather to her, too, but she needed that to make things up to Dad. Same thing with the plant for Mom. The fridge might've been nice, but it wasn't nearly as precious as those items. Paisley hoped they'd agree.

Mia smiled until Mrs. Pendlebury walked outside. "Mia Pendlebury! What in the world have you done to my yard and your clothes?"

Mia had helped them, and Paisley wanted to help her now. "Mia found an important fossil. You should be proud of her."

Mrs. Pendlebury scoffed at the tooth fossil. "You are trouble, young lady," Mrs. Pendlebury said to Paisley.

Paisley tried to not to laugh in her face. Mrs. Pendlebury had no clue. Theropods were the real trouble.

Mia stood a little taller as her mom marched her inside for a bath. Mrs. Pendlebury gave the tooth fossil another glance.

Ben's stomach grumbled louder than ever.

"I've been looking for you two and the fridge," Dad

said as he walked outside. He stopped and stared at the mangled refrigerator.

"We have a lot to explain, but that fridge is now an artifact. It is also missing a tray," Paisley said. "Here is a Mesozoic peace offering." She held out the feather.

Dad ran his hands over the gouges in the refrigerator and stared at the feather. He usually had a lot to say, but he was speechless for quite a while.

"I need to talk to you about safety while we eat dinner," Dad said. "And you better tell me and your mother everything."

Dad said nothing about Paisley being grounded … yet.

The Atoms house seemed much more comfortable and cozy as Ben and Paisley walked inside. She couldn't wait to go to school tomorrow, though she didn't care about proving anyone wrong anymore. Not even Whitney-Raelynn.

Paisley could now easily picture prehistoric Roarington as well as the dinosaurs that used to roam the land. There was still a lot to learn about dinosaurs, but Paisley had a whole new appreciation for them. And for being alive, after surviving a few dangerous encounters with them.

She still didn't think dinosaurs were terrible, though. At least not when she could only see them in books.

Science Alliance!
Make a Dinosaur Model

Like Paisley and Ben, you can make your own dinosaur model using objects like paper towel rolls, toilet paper rolls, and craft sticks to use as the bone structure. Then use modeling clay or play dough to create the body of your dinosaur. You can add a layer of skin using tissue paper or recycled bags. You might decide to paint your model. Don't forget to add details like scales, feathers, or bristles if you desire!

You can also create your own steel wool experiment like Ben did in the story.

Materials:
- steel wool
- vinegar
- thermometer (not digital)
- glass jar with a lid (large enough for the thermometer and steel wool to fit inside)

Step 1
Set the thermometer in the glass jar for several minutes to get a base reading.

Step 2
Place the piece of steel wool in the glass jar.

Step 3
Pour a layer of vinegar over the steel wool. Let it sit for a minute.

Step 4
Remove the vinegar and wrap the steel wool around the bulb of the thermometer.

Step 5
Set the steel wool and thermometer back in the jar. Close the lid and wait five minutes.

Step 6
Take the temperature again to see if there is an increase in the temperature from the chemical reaction.

Women in Science

Mary Anning was a world-famous fossil collector and paleontologist known for important finds she made in Jurassic marine fossil beds in the cliffs along the English Channel. Mary Anning's discoveries were some of the most significant geological finds of all time. Her findings led to critical changes in scientific thinking about prehistoric life and the history of life on Earth.

Mary Anning (1799–1847)

Author Q & A

Q: What dinosaur do you wish you could travel back in time to study?

A: The *Seismosaurus* to see the enormous size, and to hear the sonic boom of its tail whipping—from a safe distance!

Q: Do you think the *T. Rex* had feathers?

A: I think it might've had featherlike "filamentous feathers."

Q: What is your writing process like?

A: I write out a plot summary and then an outline. I draft the story, and then set it aside for a bit before several rounds of editing.

Silly Science!

Q: What do you call a couple of dinosaurs after they ran into each other?

A: Tyrannosaurus wrecks!

Q: What is a good nickname for a sleeping dinosaur?

A: A dino-snore

Websites to Visit

Lots of dinosaur information:

http://paleobiology.si.edu/dinosaurs/info/
everything/what.html

All about theropods:

www.ucmp.berkeley.edu/diapsids/saurischia/
theropoda.html

For dinosaur games and videos:

http://discoverykids.com/category/dinosaurs

Guess What?!

Scientists in China discovered a dinosaur, *Zhenyuanlong suni,* with large wings, talons, and lots of sharp teeth similar to the dinosaur Paisley and Ben see in the story. This discovery is especially important because it is the largest dinosaur ever found with such well-preserved bird-like wings and feathers. The fossil could help researchers better understand the connection between birds and dinosaurs.

About the Author

J.L. Anderson's education inspired her to become an author, but she thought seriously about becoming a biologist, and she once was the president of the science club in high school. She lives outside of Austin, Texas with her husband, daughter, and two naughty dogs. You can learn more about her at www.jessicaleeanderson.com.

About the Illustrator

Alan Brown's love of comic art, cartoons and drawing has driven him to follow his dreams of becoming an artist. His career as a freelance artist and designer has allowed him to work on a wide range of projects, from magazine illustration and game design to children's books. He's had the good fortune to work on comics such as *Ben 10* and *Bravest Warriors*. Alan lives in Newcastle with his wife, sons and dog.